DREAM
RESCUERS

Jennifer Lloyd
Illustrations by **Eden Cooke**

SIMPLY READ BOOKS

Help Wanted

RUBY could not believe it. Another F! Maybe she had looked too quickly. She peeked down at her job report once again. Sure enough, it still said F. F was for *Fail* in her latest tooth pick-up mission. In fact, it was her third F. This meant that she could no longer be a Tooth Fairy.

It was true—once again she had returned without a tooth. It was not her fault. A little dog had been curled up in a basket beside the boy's bed. She had been okay with the dog when he had been sleeping, but her wing flapping had caused it to wake. She had heard stories from other Tooth Fairies about dogs jumping, barking and even nipping. How could she be expected to fly over a creature that did that? It was simply too frightening! Without retrieving the tooth, she had backed away from the bed and the sleeping boy in a hurry.

Once more her fears had gotten in her way. And now, she was faced with something even more terrifying—starting over! Tooth Delivery was her world, all that she had ever known. It wouldn't seem so frightening if someone else was starting over too but all the other Tooth Fairies seemed to be successful at their missions. They were always proudly presenting their teeth to the Head Tooth Deliverer. The other Tooth Fairies didn't have any patience for her. Every time she messed up, it meant more work for them.

Ruby knew that everyone on Cloud 98 had work to do. She needed to find a new way to be useful too. What could she possibly be good at? She was not sure so she decided to sit and think. Looking around her, she spotted a newspaper stand. *Of course*, thought Ruby, *Cloud 98 News*. She remembered seeing ads for jobs in the newspaper. She rushed to pick up a copy. Ruby leafed past Super Hero rescue stories. She passed reports about Fairy Godmothers granting difficult wishes. Quickly, she flipped past tales of successful tooth pickups. Finally, at the very back, she found the *Cloud 98 News* "Help Wanted" section.

There was only one ad. Ruby read it:

DREAM RESCUERS WANTED
Please come for an interview on
December 29th at 8:00 p.m.
Department of Dream Rescue
1 Counting Sheep Lane, Cloud 98

Today was December 29th. Ruby looked at her watch. It was nearly 8:00 p.m. She had to hurry. She had never ever been to the Department of Dream Rescue. Yet, she did remember passing a little sign pointing to Counting Sheep Lane on one of her tooth pick-up missions. Luckily, it was not far. She knew she had to take Sandman's Avenue, then a left on Sweet Dreams Road. Off to the right of Sweet Dreams was the sign for Counting Sheep Lane.

Flying down the lane, she searched for the Department of Dream Rescue but did not see it. She turned the bend. A tall building jutted high into the sky. It was grey, the same color as the clouds, making it almost seem invisible. The only thing that glimmered was a tiny gold sign, which read, *Department of Dream Rescue.*

She looked up at the gigantic, unfamiliar building. Her hand trembled as she grasped the door handle. So many questions filled her

head. *What is this place? What do Dream Rescuers do? Do you need to be brave to do this job? I need a new start. I need this job,* she told herself. Taking a deep breath, Ruby found the courage to turn the door handle and let herself in.

Inside, was a small room with three chairs. The other two were filled, so Ruby slipped into the chair closest to the door. To her left, sat a deer with spiraling antlers. Strangely, he was wearing a red sweater and he kept tapping one of his hooves.

Beside the deer, sat a tiny man with a letter M on his shirt. He was so small that his feet swung under the chair, unable to touch the ground. However, he wore a cape that draped nearly to the floor.

Ruby sat and watched the clock.

TAP, TAP, went the deer.

"Please stop!" said the tiny man, in a voice that was surprisingly loud for someone so little.

"Are you talking to me?" asked Ruby.

"No! I am talking to the deer! He's driving me crazy with all of his tapping!"

"Sorry," said the deer. "I can't help it. I just need to move. It's hard for me to keep still."

As he spoke, Ruby noticed the deer had red and green bells around his neck, practically hidden by his sweater.

"Are you a reindeer?" she asked.

"Yes," said the deer.

"Why aren't you at the North Pole with Santa Claus?"

"I used to be a North Pole reindeer, but I found it too hard to keep still when I was harnessed to the sleigh. Last Christmas Eve, while Santa was loading up, I started kicking

my hooves. Just a little at first but it felt so good to move that my kicks got higher and higher, and before I knew it, the sleigh over- turned and all of the toys fell out. Santa was not happy."

The reindeer looked like he was going to cry.

"Poor you," said Ruby, leaning over to give him a pat. "I need a new start too. I was a Tooth Fairy, until I failed at too many missions."

"Sorry to hear that. My name is Ralph, by the way," he answered, offering one of his hooves to shake.

"I'm Ruby."

Ruby turned to the tiny man. "Why are you here?" she asked.

"Mighty's the name. I wasn't taken se- riously at my last job at Super Hero Rescue

Services. No one even used my real name. Instead, I got called Little Shrimp or Pea-Sized. Everyone was always rushing around, admiring the bigger, taller Super Heroes. They would step on my cape and knock me over. I was never even given a chance to battle villains."

What a sad story, thought Ruby. She was about to say something comforting when, across the room, a door opened.

2

Oscar

RUBY looked at the clock above the door. It read exactly 8:00 p.m.

A man with the tidiest hair Ruby had ever seen entered the room. He was wearing a shiny white lab coat and carrying a clipboard.

"My name is Oscar. I am the Head of Dream Rescue. Are you all here about the Dream Rescue job?" he asked in a friendly voice.

Mighty straightened his cape and stood up on the seat of his chair. "Yes," he said, his voice booming even louder than before.

Ralph's chair wobbled as he scrambled to greet Oscar. "Yes," he answered too.

Who is this Oscar? wondered Ruby. *He sounds friendly, but is he a good Head? He carries a clipboard like the Head Tooth Deliverer, but he doesn't look anything like her.* The Head Tooth Deliverer's hair was long and flowing. Her dress was full of flashy sparkles, unlike Oscar's plain coat.

"Yes," Ruby finally responded.

Oscar took a silver pen from behind his ear. As they each said their names, he recorded them with lightning speed.

"Did anyone else come?" Oscar asked.

"No," said Mighty, in his booming voice.

Mighty was now standing on tiptoe.

He must be trying to look taller to impress Oscar, thought Ruby.

She glanced over at Ralph. He had stopped tapping. He stood with his back hooves crossed, one holding down the other.

If Oscar is asking if anyone else came, he must think that we're not right for the job. He's probably already guessed that I'm not brave.

At last, Oscar spoke, "You don't look like my usual Dream Rescuers. But I know from dreams that things are not always as they seem."

Ruby held her breath. *What does Oscar mean?* she wondered.

But he didn't explain. Instead, mysteriously, a pocket watch slipped from under Oscar's coat sleeve into one of his hands. He looked at it and frowned. "Three minutes after eight. I can't wait any longer. I need a new team. Perhaps if you work well together, I'll try you out."

A grin broke out across Ruby's face. *He's giving us a chance!*

"Come this way," said Oscar.

Mighty scurried down from his chair, his cape swishing behind him. Ralph followed closely.

"Off my cape!" Mighty said to Ralph.

"Sorry," said Ralph. "I was just trying to keep up."

Ruby walked behind. Oscar led them into a very large room with a high ceiling. Inside, was a giant machine with many colored buttons. Attached to it, was a screen as tall as the wall.

Ruby started reading the screen:

CHILD NAME:	TYPE OF FEAR:
MAJA	DOGS
JACOB	MONSTERS
AMÉLIE	DARKNESS
TARKAN	BIRDS
EMMA	DRAGONS
OLIVIA	DENTISTS
JUAN	BUGS
AVA	CLOWNS
AMARE	GHOSTS
SANDER	BURGLARS
DANIEL	SHARKS
KATIA	VOLCANOS
EDUARDO	SPIDERS
AIKA	DOLLS
KWANG-MIN	DINOSAURS
JAMIR	BATS
KYOKO	STORMS
AISLING	SNAKES
ANNUSHKA	HEIGHTS
MASSIMO	FLYING

She kept reading down the screen, but as she read the list grew longer and longer. Ruby couldn't keep up. There are so many names and such scary sounding fears.

"This machine shows us the children who need help and the nightmares they're having," said Oscar.

Ruby shuddered. *Those nightmares do sound frightening.*

Mighty seemed to have a different opinion. "Why would anyone be frightened of a doll?" he asked.

"Oh, dolls can be very scary, especially the ones that talk. As you fly overhead, you never know what they will blurt out," answered Ruby. However, she could tell that Mighty was not convinced.

"What exactly does a Dream Rescuer do?" she asked Oscar, trying to change the subject.

"You don't know?" said Oscar.

"No," said Ruby, feeling a bit foolish.

"I'm not so sure myself," said Mighty, "but if it involves rescuing, I'm up for the challenge."

"I don't know either," admitted Ralph. "I guess we all just needed a job."

Ruby felt a little better, as she waited for Oscar to explain.

3

Dream Rescuer Goggles

"D REAM Rescuers fly down to the houses of human children. They help children who are having nightmares. They solve their dreams for them, so that they can sleep peacefully again," explained Oscar.

"Why do Dream Rescuers have to solve the children's dreams?" asked Mighty. "Why don't they just wake them up instead?"

"It's not that simple. If you just wake up the children, the next time they sleep, they will have the same nightmare all over again. You have to fix it for them, so their nightmares will go away," answered Oscar.

"How do Dream Rescuers get into a child's dream to fix it?" asked Ralph.

"Did you know that dreams are really giant bubbles? The bubbles float above humans' heads while they're sleeping," explained Oscar.

"I never saw any floating bubbles when I was trying to do tooth pick-ups," said Ruby.

"That's because you weren't wearing Dream Rescuer goggles."

Oscar went to a cupboard and pulled out a pair of funny-looking glasses with stretchable bands attached.

"Awesome! Can I try on a pair?" asked Ralph.

"Yes, of course," Oscar said. He opened the cupboard wider. There, in extremely neat rows, sat dozens of Dream Rescuer goggles. Oscar picked out two more.

Mighty pushed in front and took his pair first. He held up the lenses to the light, as if trying to figure out how they worked.

Ralph grabbed the next pair. He stretched the band and tried to fit it over his head, but it got stuck on one of his antlers. He pulled harder.

"Careful. The goggles are fragile!" said Oscar.

At last, Ralph got them on. "I don't see any dream bubbles," he said. He started prancing around the room, looking up and then looking down.

"Oh, they only work when you're near someone sleeping. The goggles let you see the faint outline of the dream. And if you look closely, you'll see a dark spot on one side of the bubble. That's the portal to get into the dream. By the way, can you all fly?"

"As fast as the wind," said Mighty, flapping his cape.

"That's how I pulled Santa's sleigh," said Ralph. As he spoke, he kicked his back legs and began to rise a little in the air.

"Not now, Ralph," said Oscar.

"I can fly too," said Ruby, carefully taking the third pair of glasses from Oscar.

"Good. Since the dream bubble floats, you'll have to fly up to it. Next, you'll need to find the dark spot and go through it. Once you're through, you'll instantly be part of the dream. The important thing is to remember where in the dream you came in, so you can get back out after you've solved the nightmare," continued Oscar.

As Oscar said the word nightmare, Ruby looked up at the screen again. The list of names kept getting longer and longer.

Pointing to the screen, Mighty asked, "How do you know about the nightmares?"

"It is a little bit like how Tooth Fairies know when a child has lost a tooth. All children have invisible sensors under their beds. When they're having nightmares, they usually move around a lot or call out. The sensors can decode words and movement signals, which tell what kinds of dreams the children are having. The signals are sent to this Nightmare Notifier, which makes the names of the children appear on the giant screen."

"Looks like you have lots of cases," said Ralph, tapping his hooves as he spoke.

"Yes," said Oscar, looking at his pocket watch again. "There are many children to help. Can you all start right away?"

Ruby found herself nodding yes along with the others, but deep down she wasn't sure. *This new job seems scary. It seems even more frightening than being a Tooth Fairy. Can I do this? If the children are scared of their nightmares, won't I be afraid too?*

Ruby took a deep breath. *I have to at least try.*

4

New Suits

"WHO do we rescue first?" asked Mighty. "The Nightmare Notifier will tell us," explained Oscar, bringing them closer to the giant machine. "It always knows who needs help the most."

He pressed a green button on the side of the Nightmare Notifier.

BEEP! WHIRR! It made all kinds of noises. A tube on top spouted a mist of tiny, glittering bubbles.

"Wow! What a fantastic machine!" Ralph yelled. He reached towards the green button with one of his front hooves, trying to push it again.

"Ralph!" cried Oscar, stopping him in time.

"Sorry," said Ralph. "I just wanted to see the bubbles again."

Out of a slot, came a small piece of paper.

Oscar read the name and said, "Yes, of course. I knew it would be Emma. I've been worried about her. She's nine years old and she lives in London, England. For several nights, she's been dreaming about a dragon chasing her in a castle. We need to help her in a hurry!"

"A dragon?" said Ruby, nervously.

"No problem," said Mighty. "At last, something to battle!"

"We can do it," added Ralph.

Ruby gulped.

"Let's start by giving you Dream Rescuer suits," said Oscar.

He opened a gigantic cupboard.

"I'll go first," said Mighty, taking off his boots.

"Wait, Mighty. Yours is in the next cupboard," said Oscar. "I'll begin with Ruby."

Oscar reached for a jumpsuit with a hood. The suit was as black as the dark cupboard. But when Oscar pulled it out, the strangest thing happened. Right before Ruby's eyes, the jumpsuit changed colors. It changed to yellow, the exact same yellow as the wall behind her.

"Wow! Did that suit just change color?" asked Ruby.

"Yes, Dream Rescuer suits are specially camouflaged. Wherever you walk, your suit will change to the color of what is around you, like a chameleon."

"Why is that necessary?" asked Mighty.

"Just like everyone else on Cloud 98, Dream Rescuers are invisible helpers. They try to avoid being detected by the human world."

Ruby was sad to cover her sparkly pink fairy dress but she tried on the suit. Luckily, it was a perfect fit!

"Put the hood up," said Mighty. "Stand over by the wall. I want to see what happens."

Ruby put up her hood and moved near the wall.

"Wow! I can't see you anymore!" said Mighty.

"How come Ruby doesn't look invisible to me?" asked Ralph. "I can see her clearly."

"That's because you are still wearing your goggles. Dream Rescuer goggles are specially made to see dream bubbles but they also let you see other Dream Rescuers. This allows

you to work together on your missions," said Oscar.

"Can I have my suit now?" asked Ralph, heading over to the cupboard.

"Wait, Ralph! Those suits need to be in order, so I can find the right sizes quickly," said Oscar. Then, with a wave of his hand, Oscar piled all of the suits tidily again.

Ruby was amazed. *Did that really just happen? Maybe I imagined it.* Oscar gave a suit to Ralph, who had trouble sticking his hooves through the arm holes. With some help from Ruby, he fit into it.

Farther down, Oscar opened a miniature cupboard. He pulled out a few suits for Mighty but they were much too big. He looked deep in the cupboard and found one more.

"I'm afraid this is the smallest suit we have," apologized Oscar.

Mighty didn't seem too pleased, but he put on the suit anyway. Ruby helped him roll the legs and arms and tuck his cape inside so that it wouldn't show. On went their goggles and at last they were ready.

Oscar checked his pocket watch again. "Let's get you to the Tube Transport System. It's in the basement of the building."

5

Tube Transport

THE team walked out of the yellow room and started down some blue stairs.

I wonder what Tube Transport could be? Everything about Dream Rescue is so new and different, Ruby thought.

At the bottom of the stairs, they came to a long corridor.

"Keep to the right," said Oscar. They moved over just in time. Ruby could see a suited figure coming towards them on the left.

"Excellent job handling the snake," Oscar said to the suited figure.

"Glad the monster didn't give you any trouble," Oscar said to a second suited passerby.

Ruby slowed her pace. *Who are these people passing? Why are they talking about such scary things?*

"Are there many other Dream Rescuers working here?" asked Mighty.

"Oh, yes," answered Oscar. "However, as you could see on the screen, we just can't keep up with the demand. That's why I put the ad for new Dream Rescuers in the Cloud 98 News."

More suited figures passed. Every time, Oscar spoke with them about their missions.

The other Dream Rescuers look serious.

They're tall and they have such loud, confident voices, thought Ruby. *None of them seem like me.*

They passed a door marked *South American Transport*, then a door marked, *North American Transport*. Up ahead, the *Asian Transport* door quickly closed in front of them but they did not stop. Oscar led them to the door marked, *European Transport*, instead.

This opened to a hallway, with many new doors, each with the name of a different country.

Ruby read some of them, *France, Germany, Spain, Switzerland.*

Oscar said, "The Tube Transport System continues all the way to the underground of London. When you arrive, push open the Tube Transport Exit door, which will lead

GERMANY

FRANCE

SPAIN

SWITZERLAND

AL

EUROPEAN
TRANSPORT

ITALY

ENGLAND

SCOTLAND

you right out onto Rosewood Avenue, Emma's street. Once you find her flat, number 312, fly up to Emma's room. From what I could see from the images on the Nightmare Notifier, her window is on the third floor, top north corner, and she's left it open."

With that, Oscar pushed open a door marked, *England*. A gush of wind rushed in. To Ruby's surprise, on the other side of the door was a giant, clear, tube-slide that wound downwards into the clouds below.

"The Tube Transport System is a slide?" asked Ruby. "We're sliding all of the way to England?"

"Yes, Dream Rescuers must get to their destinations quickly. Children are in need and sometimes their nightmares don't last that long. The slide is actually very quick and direct."

"Awesome! I can't wait to try it!" said Ralph.

Ruby tried to smile and agree, but she did not share Ralph's excitement.

"How do we get back?" said Mighty. "Slides go down but not up."

"Oh, easy," chuckled Oscar. "At the bottom of the slide, you'll see a button for an invisible rope pulley. Hold on tight and it'll pull you back up to this building."

Oscar started to tap some buttons on a keyboard. "Give me a minute. I just need to program the exact tilt of the slide to Rosewood Avenue." While he did this, Ralph lifted one hoof to climb in.

"Wait, Ralph!" called Mighty. "Oscar didn't tell us how to solve the nightmare. I need to know how I can battle the dragon."

"Yes, I was just about to get to that," said Oscar. "Let me find what you'll need."

Oscar dug into the pocket of his lab coat.

"Snake Repellent won't help you. No, Spider-Be-Gone won't do either. Monster Mist isn't right. Aha! Here's the one." Oscar passed a tiny green spray bottle to Mighty.

Mighty read the label to the others, "Dragon Spray: Push and hold the spray button for three full seconds. For best results, spray directly on dragon's head. Dragon will fall asleep shortly."

"Can we go now?" asked Ralph, still holding on to the top of the slide.

"Yes," said Oscar, looking at his watch once again. "You need to get to Emma."

Ruby climbed in after Ralph. She cautiously fit in behind him and held tight to his back.

"I think for Mighty's safety, he should sit on your lap," Oscar said to Ruby. "Otherwise, he might get bumped around a bit."

"On her lap!" cried Mighty. "I'm too old to sit on someone's lap!"

"Come on, Mighty! We need to get going!" urged Ralph.

With a sigh, Mighty sat down on Ruby's lap. He squirmed and wiggled.

"Good luck!" said Oscar. "I'll see you when you get back."

"You're not coming with us?" asked Ruby.

"No. I must keep things running smooth-ly... "

They didn't hear the rest of Oscar's answer, because as he had started talking, Ralph had let go of the top of the slide.

6

Downwards

AT FIRST, the slide was slow with a gradual decline and some gentle turns.

But soon, they were sliding faster and faster.

"Weeeeeeeeee!" Ralph cheered as they gained speed.

Spiraling and then straight, they passed cloud after cloud.

They went even faster!

It was too fast for Ruby! She couldn't speak. She couldn't look.

"Ruby! You are squeezing me too tight!" said Mighty.

"Sorry," whispered Ruby, not letting go. She tried to cling to Ralph as well but he kept moving around in excitement.

"Ralph, keep still," said Mighty. "You're making us bump all over!"

"Sorry! This slide is just so much fun!"

Ruby kept her eyes shut.

They zoomed so quickly that just moments later, Ralph announced, "We're getting close! I see lights!"

Ruby took a quick peek. Down below were millions of beautiful, twinkling lights.

"I can see Big Ben!" said Ralph.

"Who is Big Ben?" asked Ruby.

"It's the clock tower below. We passed it last year on Santa's sleigh."

"Almost there!" announced Mighty, watching the route ahead. "Looks like we're about to go underground!"

Right through the twinkling lights, they zoomed, down into a dark tunnel below the city. The slide continued flat until they slowed at last.

Excited, but a little dazed, the team stood up and walked out of the slide. A few feet ahead, they found a door marked, *Tube Transport Exit*. Ralph pushed it open.

"Hold on!" said Ruby. "Ralph, your hood has fallen down. You'll be visible!"

She got Ralph sorted out and then they stepped onto the dark street.

Mighty checked the street sign on the corner. "Rosewood Avenue," he announced.

Ralph galloped ahead down the street. Mighty and Ruby flew behind, trying to keep up.

"Watch out!" called Mighty, as a double-decker bus sped past.

"Eeeeek!" cried Ruby, leaping off the street.

When the bus moved on, they noticed the address ahead of them.

"312! " cheered Ralph.

Emma's Room

WHEN they got to Emma's building, Ruby couldn't remember what Oscar had said about Emma's window. "Do you remember, Ralph?" she asked. Ralph shook his head.

"Third floor, top north corner," interrupted Mighty.

"Let's go!" said Ralph.

Mighty hopped in the open window. Ruby went next. It was hard for Ralph to fit. He had to bend low to get his antlers in first, followed by his front and back hooves.

THUMP! Ralph landed on the floor, inside.

"Sh! Ralph, don't wake Emma!" said Ruby.

"Oops," whispered Ralph.

Squinting, the team could make out the shadows of a pretty little bedroom. It had lots of books on the shelves. A teddy bear sat on a desk. There, in a high princess bed, slept Emma.

But Emma didn't look like she was sleeping very well. She was tossing and turning.

"Help!" Emma cried out in her sleep.

"We need to help Emma in a hurry," whispered Ruby.

"But how do we do it?" asked Ralph. "I don't see her dream bubble."

"Look up!" said Mighty.

Ruby looked up. There, floating above Emma's bed, was a giant bubble.

"Wow!" said Ralph.

They flew closer. Sure enough, there was a dark spot on one side.

Up closer, they could see the dark spot was an opening, like an empty tunnel. Mighty flew through first.

Ralph went next.

Ruby flew in place, frozen. *If I go in, I'll have to meet a dragon! Then again, I won't be alone. It feels good to be part of a team and I don't want to let Mighty and Ralph down. And staying here by myself is scary too. What if Emma has a talking doll or worse? What if she has a dog?*

"Help!" cried Emma, once again.

Poor Emma! She is even more frightened than me. Ruby took a deep breath. She followed the others through the dark opening.

The Dragon

THUD! Ruby landed on the hard stone floor next to Ralph and Mighty.

She looked around. They were sprawled right next to a high, arched window. The walls were curved and also made of stone. Everything seemed very old.

"I think we're in the castle," said Mighty. "But where is Emma?"

"Help!" called a little girl's voice. It was coming from a floor below.

They headed down a windy, narrow staircase, towards the voice. At the bottom, they found themselves in a huge room with a high ceiling. Beautiful tiles covered the floor. The room had no furniture, except for a large table with chairs. A giant chandelier hung above the table.

"A ballroom!" said Ruby. "How lovely!"

At the other end of the ballroom, they spotted Emma. She was running. She was running very fast because something was chasing her. It was large. It was green. It had scales all over it and it was breathing fire!

"The dragon!" gasped Ruby. He was even bigger and scarier than she imagined.

"Pass me the dragon spray!" whispered Ralph.

"Hey! I am the Super Hero! I am supposed to battle the dragon!" cried Mighty.

"I can run faster!" said Ralph. "Let me try!"

Ralph and Mighty looked at Ruby.

"Are you coming?" asked Mighty.

Ruby trembled. Tears streamed down her cheeks. "I can't. I'm too scared! This always happens to me. That's why I failed as a Tooth Fairy," she answered.

"It's okay, Ruby," said Ralph.

Mighty scanned the room. "Wait for us under the table. You'll be safe there."

As Ralph and Mighty headed towards the dragon, Ruby flew to the table. She lifted a corner of the velvet tablecloth and ducked under. It was dark underneath. She curled herself in a ball and waited.

She did not have to wait long before Mighty joined her.

"We couldn't even get close to the dragon," he explained. "He moves too fast. His breath is too hot."

BUMP! Ralph nearly knocked a chair over as he climbed under too.

"Be careful, Ralph!" said Ruby.

Now what were they going to do?

The New Plan

"WE need a new way to spray the dragon. Does anyone have any ideas?" said Ralph.

"Ralph, by bumping the chair, you just gave me one," said Mighty. "Usually, we ask you not to move. But this time, you'll need to move. You'll need to move a lot. You'll need to move and bump the table so loudly that the dragon can hear it. He'll turn to come and see what's making all of the noise."

"What will you do?" asked Ralph.

"I'll stand in the chandelier above the table. I think that I'm just small enough to fit right in the middle between the candlesticks. The dragon won't notice me. When he comes close to the table, I'll spray him from above."

"Can I keep hiding under here?" said Ruby.

"No, Ruby. You'll need to make sure that I've made it safely onto the chandelier. You'll have to come out from under the table and climb up onto one of the dining chairs to get a good view. When I'm in position and ready, I'll give you a thumb's-up signal. That means that you can go back under the table to tell Ralph to start moving," said Mighty.

"Why can't I just come out and check for your thumbs-up signal instead?" asked Ralph.

"Ralph, you know how you get restless. I need Ruby to make sure that you don't start moving early," explained Mighty.

"Okay," said Ralph. Ruby nodded too. She was not so sure of Mighty's plan, but at least she didn't have to spray the dragon herself.

"I'm on my way," said Mighty.

Ruby stayed put for a few seconds. *It's so much safer under the table.*

"Go on, Ruby. We need you," nudged Ralph.

Lifting the tablecloth, Ruby cautiously stepped out. She checked and saw that the dragon was still chasing Emma on the other side of the room. Swiftly, she climbed up onto the nearest chair.

Hurry, Mighty! Please get to the chandelier quickly!

She watched as Mighty reached the chandelier above. He seemed to be having a hard time balancing. The chandelier started to swing as he squeezed between the candles. Mighty wobbled. Ruby knew that he was not ready yet.

But beside her, the table started to shake. She darted back.

"Not yet, Ralph! Keep still. Mighty hasn't given me the signal."

Ralph crossed his back hooves, one holding down the other.

Reluctantly, Ruby climbed back onto the chair. She looked up at Mighty, who seemed to now be balanced perfectly. He was holding the spray ready to go. He nodded at Ruby and gave her a thumbs- up.

Down she went again. Peeking under the tablecloth, she told Ralph, "Now!"

Ralph started to move again. He shook. He bumped. He kicked. The table lifted and landed *THUD! BOOM! THUD! THUD! BOOM!* His hooves kicked forwards and backwards. The table lifted and landed some more. *THUD! THUD! BOOM! BOOM! BOOM!*

"Yikes!" cried Ruby, as one of Ralph's hooves swung close to where she was crouched.

I can't stay here. I'll be safer on the chair.

But this time, when Ruby climbed back up, she could see that Mighty's plan was working. Gigantic dragon feet were approaching!

Eek! Trembling, she glanced hopefully up at Mighty.

He looks ready! He will save the day! But wait! Why is the chandelier swinging so much? Are the vibrations from the dragon's feet causing it to wobble? Hold on, Mighty! Ruby watched as the spray slipped from Mighty's hands and tumbled down onto the table. It stopped right in front of her chair.

"Oh no!" cried Mighty. The dragon lifted his head, at the sound of Mighty's voice.

Taking a deep breath, Ruby reached and grabbed the spray.

Hold tight to the spray! Just think of the others! Whatever you do, don't look down at the dragon.

She flew upwards. And as she did, she could hear Mighty shouting at her, "Ruby, push the button!"

There was no time to hand the spray to Mighty. The dragon was too close. She was the one in perfect position, right above the dragon's head!

I have to do this!

Pushing the button, Ruby counted three seconds. The blue mist drifted out of the bottle and covered the dragon's face! The dragon started to sway. He closed his eyes. He let out a big sigh, before falling to the floor. And when he did, he started to snore—a deep, very loud dragon snore!

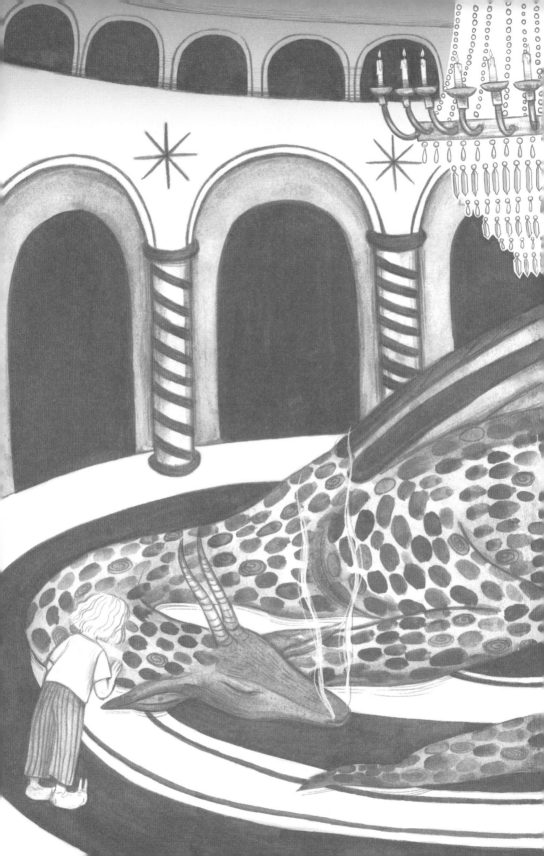

10

Heading Back

RALPH, Mighty and Ruby stood beside the dragon. They wanted to congratulate each other, but they couldn't. They needed to stay very, very quiet. Someone was standing nearby.

It was Emma. "The dragon is asleep? How can that be? I must have tired him out with all of that running. I am safe! Hurray!" she said, with a smile.

Quietly, she tiptoed to the edge of the ballroom and opened a door leading outside. Out
she went, skipping happily.

"Let's go," said Mighty. "We need to get to
the portal before the dragon wakes up."

Up the spiral staircase they ran, back to
the arched window where they came in.

THUD! They each landed back in Emma's
room.

To their astonishment, Emma was sleeping soundly in her bed. She looked peaceful
and happy.

Out the window they flew, back to the
tube-slide.

Mighty looked for the button to get them up.
At last, he spotted a purple button, marked,
"Invisible Pulley. Hold tight at all times."

Mighty pushed it, and strangely enough,
they could not see it, but a rope could be felt
in their hands.

"Hold on!" he told them. Mighty pushed another button marked, *"Start,"* and up they were pulled. As they rose, Ruby kept her eyes open. She enjoyed the view of London's sparkling lights, twinkling below. Ralph chatted happily, but Mighty stayed very quiet.

"Are you okay, Mighty?" Ruby asked.

"I'm disappointed. I wish I hadn't dropped the spray. I was a terrible Super Hero and now I am a terrible Dream Rescuer."

"Mighty, if it hadn't been for your fantastic plan, we never would've been able to save Emma," said Ruby, gently.

"Thanks, Ruby. I guess that we all played a part," answered Mighty.

At the top of the slide, Oscar was there to greet them.

"You did it!" he said. "You've proven that you can be Dream Rescuers. Come back tomorrow night and you can help someone else."

Ralph, Mighty and Ruby started walking towards the stairs.

"Wait!" said Oscar. "I nearly forgot."

He passed a report to each one of them. Ruby was afraid to look. She waited for the others to go ahead. When she was all alone, she peeked.

The first thing she spotted was an F. But this time the F was not for the word *Fail* but instead for the word *Finished*, as she had *"Finished a mission!"*

Waving her report, Ruby hurried to catch up to the others. She felt happy and proud.

I did it! I really did it! I was able to help solve a nightmare!

Ruby could hardly wait to start her next mission, even if it meant facing another scary nightmare. Somehow, thanks to Oscar, Mighty and Ralph, everything seemed possible.

First published in 2021 by Simply Read Books Inc
Text copyright 2021 Jennifer Lloyd
Illustrations copyright 2021 Eden Cooke

LIBRARY AND ARCHIVES CANADA CATALOGUING IN PUBLICATION

Title: Dream rescuers / Jennifer Lloyd ; illustrated by Eden Cooke.
Names: Lloyd, Jennifer, author. | Cooke, Eden, illustrator.
Identifiers: Canadiana 20200337343 | ISBN 9781927018927 (hardcover)
Classification: LCC PS8623.L69 D74 2021 | DDC jC813/.6—dc23

We gratefully acknowledge for their financial support of our
publishing program the Canada Council for the Arts, the BC Arts
Council, and the Government of Canada.

Manufactured in Korea
Book design by Naomi MacDougall and Carolina Rocha

10 9 8 7 6 5 4 3 2 1

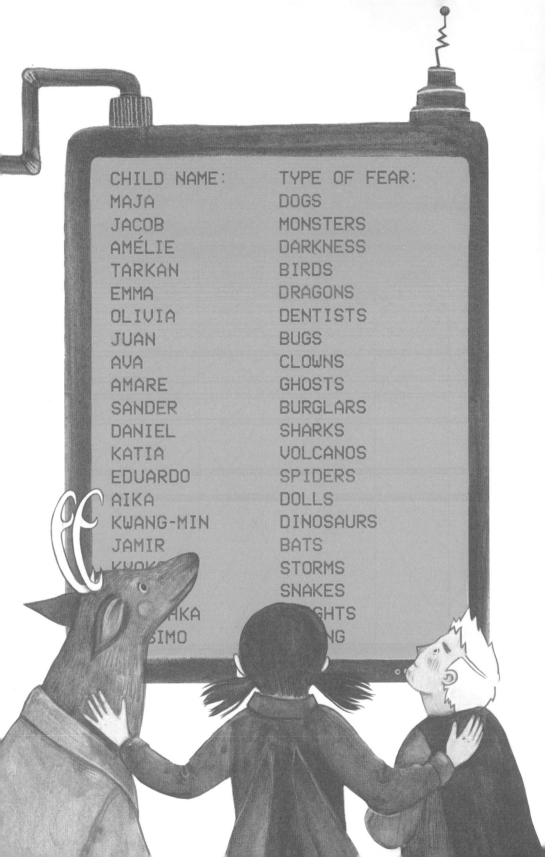